Gone But Not Forgotten

The Strength of a Woman

Written by

Crystal Laurent

Laurent Publishing

P.O. Box 431

Hiram, GA. 30141

www.CrystalKaye.com

ISBN: 978-1-7371425-0-8 © 2021 by Crystal Laurent

I dedicate this book to all the young women across the world. I am you and you are me. Never let your circumstances determine your future. God never makes mistakes and will never leave you.

Acknowledgments

Special thanks to the special person in my life who inspired me along this journey. I would have never completed this without your inspiration and encouragement. It takes a lot to live in your truth, face insecurities, and to allow yourself to finally heal.

Preface

I created this book to show an account of life struggles a lot of women endure from childhood to adulthood. As women, we often deal with things we are too ashamed to speak about, such as sexual abuse, domestic violence, and depression. To break the cycle and reclaim ourselves, we must first face the torments of our past and begin the healing process. Only when we heal ourselves do we discover our voice. Here is Keisha's journey to discovering hers, in hopes that her story will encourage others to tell theirs.

Table of Contents

Chapter One

The Creation

eing a woman, they compare you to a rose. Something that smells sweet, looks beautiful, and is the idea of perfection. What people don't notice are the thorns that grow as a reminder of the scars we endured in life to get us where we are today. To grasp the concept, you must first understand where it started.

It all started in the summer of June 1985, when a beautiful girl was born and given to the perfect family. Bullshit! That story never existed. Hi, my name is Keisha, and I'm going to tell you the actual story. I was born into a family of chaos, drugs, violence, and everything else that the ghetto could bring. My life was not that of the typical young girl living in New Orleans, full of second lines and parties. You would think of New Orleans as being one of the coolest places to live. Let me break it to you—for me, it wasn't. Growing up here can be a veritable nightmare. It is the survival of the fittest.

I was born into a family of five. My mom had three girls and one boy. I was the last child, or what we can refer to as the "runt of the litter." My mother was a single parent, and, growing up, my father wasn't around. What little I knew about their relationship was that they were high school sweethearts gone wrong. They met in the high school band and became boyfriend and girlfriend. During their brief courtship, my mom found out she was pregnant with my oldest sister at fifteen. The way the story goes, they both dropped out of school. My dad enlisted in the military, my mom had my sister, and soon they got married. Within a few years, they also had my other sister and my brother. Their marriage didn't last, and they ended up getting a divorce. Although they divorced, they still slept with each other and had another baby—me. Because of the off-and-on-again relationship, this led to him always questioning whether I was his. I would often hear them arguing over the difference in how he treated my siblings compared to me. The arguments would be over him picking up my brother and sister for trips, while leaving me behind. As a kid, I thought little of it, except I knew I wasn't the wanted child. However, my great-grandmother and grandmother would come to pick me up as if they were trying to compensate for him not fully accepting me.

Anyway, we were your typical impoverished family and lived in a one-bedroom shotgun house. Although Mom dropped out of high school and had very little education, she worked several mediocre jobs just to get by. You would think with all the jobs she had she could make millions, but there was never sufficient money to go around. It didn't help that she built up a drinking problem. Still, even though we were poor, my mom never qualified for any funded housing or even food stamp programs. Instead, we would go to a food pantry every weekend and pick up what they called the "Commodity Food." For those old enough, you know what I am talking about. We would receive a silver can that had either the word "beef" or "pork" printed on it, a block of cheese, and dry milk. That cheese was the best damn cheese I ever tasted, still is, to this day. Hell, I wonder if they still make it!

Every day, Mom would bring my siblings and me to our paternal grandmother's house while she worked. My grandmother lived in the "jets," a.k.a. the projects. For those that are a little bougie, it's government housing. This was rather our routine for many years. She didn't take us around our maternal side of the family often, as some of them treated us terribly.

Going to our maternal grandmother's house was considered a punishment. She would wake us up at four in the morning and make us read books we couldn't understand, from start to finish. If you looked as if you were going back to sleep, she would get her stick and hit you with it. Then she would deliberately feed us tiny amounts of food and tell us not to ask for more. In the evenings, she would often tell us we would never amount to anything, along with referring to us as "them project kids." She would mention this out of her anger toward our mother for choosing to be with our father. She saw him as being beneath her. Being around her was psychological torture. I hate to admit it, but when she died, there was not a tear shed from me. I just asked the Lord for forgiveness as I sat in the pew during her funeral.

Since money was always tight, we would go without some basic needs, such as heat or electricity. When things got desperate and we lost our house, we moved in with one of my mom's sisters until she could get back on her feet. This would be something that happened twice in my life, but the last time would be a time that would change me forever. It would be a period where my innocence went away and my normal life turned into turmoil. I was eight and my mom couldn't afford to rent a house of her own, so they split my siblings and me up. While my siblings lived with other relatives, my mom and I moved in with my aunt Pam and her family.

She had a husband named Will. Together, they only had one child, named Will Jr. All my life, they were what we considered the cool auntie and uncle who allowed all the kids to have fun all the time. They would have house parties, card games, and all kinds of stuff going on. For me, the idea of moving into their two-bedroom house in the Hollygrove in New Orleans's 17th Ward was going to be the shit! However, moving in that house with them would forever change me. As I came to learn, sometimes the people you consider family are nothing more than wolves in sheep's clothing. It went from being a house of fun to a house of horror.

When we moved in, everything was perfect. I met new friends that would play with me, and I got to know my big cousin. However, as time passed, I noticed that the friendly cousin was not so friendly. Will Jr. was four years older than I and was into all kinds of stuff, or what we considered just "out there." After staying with my aunt and uncle for about a month, my cousin started looking at me funny. He would ask me all kinds of questions, such as if I liked boys. It was odd because I was a huge tomboy and didn't pay attention to any boys. At least not in *that* way. All I wanted to do was play basketball and football with them. However, he would make brief comments about my body, saying things like, "You are getting breasts!" As an eight-year-old girl, no one had ever explained to me what the signs of inappropriate behavior were. I decided not to tell anyone what happened and just shrugged it off as he was just teasing me. Even though his stares and comments would continue, I kept shrugging it off, thinking he was just weird.

One night, our parents left to attend a card game and left my cousin in charge of watching us for the night. Right after they left, my cousin told me to go to bed. Because he was the oldest, and I feared him, I did what I was told. I lay in the bed pretending to be asleep, and then I heard someone enter the room. Soon after entering the room, they sat at the end of the bed. I pulled the covers from my head and noticed it was my cousin sitting there just staring at me. Abruptly, he told me, "Hey, little cousin, I need you to do me a favor." I replied, "Sure, what you need me to do?" As I looked more closely at him, I noticed that he had pulled his penis out of his pants. I had learned little about the anatomy of girls and boys. I just kept looking and wondered what it was since I did not have that body part, followed by wondering what was going to happen.

As he pulled out his penis, he whispered, "Come here." I sat up and moved closer to him. He started stroking it and uttered, "Put this in your mouth." So I told him, "No!" He said, "You don't want to get into trouble and catch a whipping, right?" I said I didn't. He said, "Well, come put it in your mouth." I just sat there, frozen. Soon after, he took my head and forced his penis into my mouth. I cried in hopes that someone would hear me and come to my rescue, but no one ever came.

After he continued to move my head up and down, white stuff sprouted from his penis, and he eventually stopped. He stood up and said that if I told anyone, no one would believe me and he would "beat the fuck out of me every day." He told me to go wash my face. I was terrified to say a word. This became something that happened to me every night while living with my aunt.

About three months had passed, and I was still enduring this torture. One day, my mom came home early from being out and caught us. Seeing my mother's face, I felt that this was my moment; she had come to my rescue. I bet some of you may think, *Thank God someone caught his ass and came to save her.* Sorry to disappoint you, but that fairytale bullshit was a dream. Before I knew it, my mom grabbed me by my hair, dragged me down the hall, and threw me in the bathroom. She began beating the hell out of me with anything that touched her hands. She hit me with the plunger, mop, her hand, extension cord, and, hell, the soap too. Once the beating was over, my mom called and told my aunt and uncle what happened. They put me in the room, then scolded and blamed me for everything. I was told I was being "fast." All the while, nothing happened to my cousin. He received no punishment at all. This is the moment I changed from an innocent girl to being reclusive and trying to hide from the world. My appearance changed. I would wear my brother's clothes or whatever I could find to hide my body. It made me feel safe, as if no one would notice me. And in one fell swoop, I learned family doesn't mean *shit*!

Once the drama was over, my mom shipped me to my maternal grandmother's house and left me to live there for a couple of months. Her leaving me there made me feel as if I had been abandoned. I guess you may wonder why I didn't stay with my mother. Well, my mother had issues besides just her drinking habit. She would also get into relationships in which the men she chose didn't want her to have her kids around. Often, she would choose them over us. It didn't help that these types of men would beat and then leave her.

You see, not only was there shit at home, but more drama started once they enrolled me in elementary school. School in New Orleans was hell, and my classmates bullied me. Kids would make fun of my looks, size, and clothes. Being from there and living in the hood, reading and writing weren't what we needed to learn. Fighting 101 was part of the curriculum, and I was darn good at it. I guess being in the projects had its perks. Every day, I fought, and I did not discriminate. I fought people from eight to eighty, male or female. Hell, anybody could get it. By the time I was thirteen, I was out there, wild in the streets. I linked up with some fellas in the neighborhood and became the girl that held their drugs. As for my home life, it was nonexistent. I was what society considered a runaway. I was so far out there that I would steal clothes out of stores. Hell, I had gotten so bold, I started hitting up the shoe store too. I did it thinking I was untouchable.

In true bad-girl fashion, shit caught up with me. It all ended when I got caught stealing the littlest item, socks. Out of all the shit I have stolen in my life, fucking socks is what I get caught with! They took me out of the mall in handcuffs. Yes, embarrassing. I ended up going to court, where I plead guilty. Now, because I was still a minor, I had to see a judge in juvenile court so they could render any judgment. Like I said, I was a handful, and I talked back to the judge just as if he was anybody on the streets. The judge got so angry with me and said, "I should send you to LTI (the women's prison), but I'm going to give you a chance." He placed me on one-year probation, with drug testing every month. But do you think I learned my lesson? *Hell no!* Sitting in that courtroom, I didn't give a damn about what happened to me. Hell, I preferred prison over living on the streets. I knew he mentioned that shit to scare me, but I was like, *Fuck it, just give me what you were going to give me, so I can go.* In my mind, I was still going to do me, just be smarter about it.

A year passed and my probation was up, so I went to do what I knew best: hang out and get money. I graduated with the dope dealers and now they would let me see a little more action. I saw how they cut it up and everything. They let me hold the dope for them because the police never checked the women. The one rule they gave me if I ever got caught was to never tell, but just take the loss. So that's what I did for the next six months—until I almost got caught. I will never forget that day. I was on the block when one guy I called "Uncle" said, "Hold these three twenties for me, the police are riding through." I had done this regularly, but this time was different. You know how you get that feeling that something is about to go down? Well, that's the feeling I had.

As we were standing there, they pulled up out of nowhere. Back then, we called them the "jump-off boys." They shook people down, so I tried to play it off as though I wasn't with them. But as I walked farther away, one officer called me over and I ran. I ran as if I was in the damn Olympics, jumping fences like they were hurdles! It was as if I had scary speed superpowers. Next thing I knew, I was ducking in alleys and hiding in abandoned houses. After that experience, it was the last time that I did that! Here I am, a thirteen-year-old girl that had been out in the street life. The only thing I learned was that I wasn't about to keep running from the police for something that wasn't mine. Fuck the street code of taking the loss. Even at a young age, I developed some common sense and realized that wasn't how I wanted to live my life. It's funny how, although I was in the streets, I still would get up and go to school every day. I would go to school as if nothing ever happened.

Now, I said I went to school, but I was still a handful. By the time I made it to the eighth grade, they expelled me three times in one year, for fighting. It was to the point I could not return to any Orleans Parish school and found myself in front of another judge. This time, I was ordered to attend an alternative school. I didn't even care. While leaving court, I ran into a girl who was a friend of my aunt's named Keedy. She and my aunt were close friends and five years older than me. Since she and my aunt were close, I hung out with her. I thought this would have been a genuine friendship that would last ages, but the future had unique plans.

Keedy and I started hanging out every day, all day. When I didn't have anywhere to go, I would stay with her by her grandfather's house uptown. While hanging out uptown, we spent our day chilling in the Magnolia Projects hard. This was where we met two other girls she claimed were her cousins, Shorty and Rhonda.

These girls were much wilder than I was. Their hustle was to finesse dudes out of their money. When I think back on it, they were underage prostitutes. I never took part in what they were getting into, because it petrified me being around men given my experience of the molestation by my cousin. To be clear, I liked boys and found them attractive, but I was terrified to let any of them touch me. The extent of my physical interactions with them was saying "what's up" and giving them a handshake.

However, hanging with these girls seemed cool because we got into some of the same shit. We were all out hustling for money any way we could get it. One day, we were so broke that we sat down and discussed what I now consider to be the unthinkable. All of us were so desperate and needed money, we thought out a plan to rob Keedy's grandpa. Her grandpa was an older man and only received an SSI check once a month. Not thinking of any repercussions, I was down. On the day we planned to rob him, we pulled up to the house and I knocked on the door. Keedy yelled, "Grandpa, let me in! It's Keisha and Keedy." When her grandpa opened the door, we walked in pretending that we were there to check on him. We walked around the house, casing our surroundings. Her grandpa's name was Mr. James. As we sat down, he told us, "Let me go to the bathroom and I will be right back." We were like, "Okay," then looked at each other and decided that when he came back, we were going to just do it. A few seconds later, in that moment, while waiting, a little feeling came over me that said, *Do not make this decision.* It was a feeling that was so overpowering, it made me back out. I looked at Keedy and said, "I cannot do this. This is not right." This man had let me stay in his home when I had nowhere to go. She looked back at me and said, "Okay, I feel you." I got up and left the house. Thinking back, I'm so glad that I didn't go through with it. I would not have been able to live with myself. After that day, I decided this lifestyle was not the one for me. I wasn't sure if Keedy was mad at me for backing out, but if she was, she didn't let it show.

Chapter Two

Tragedy

A couple of months passed after the incident. It was Mardi Gras in New Orleans, and you know what that means . . . time to hit Bourbon Street and party! Keedy and I were still hanging out together. We were becoming best friends. I ended up letting her convince me to go hang out where the action was. We didn't have transportation and had to catch an RTA (public bus) to get there. We made it and joined the crowd. It was full of people from all over the world. There was music blasting, people drinking, and women taking off their clothes, showing their breast for beads. Of course, I wasn't one of those that fell for the show-your-titties-for-beads bullshit. I was too busy checking which club we could sneak into that wasn't checking IDs. When partying in New Orleans during Mardi Gras, clubs just let anyone in, as long as you were spending money.

Even though I was underage, I didn't look it. I was light-skinned, tall, slim, with huge boobs, and wore the most natural-looking grayish contacts. Most people thought I was older than I was. You could consider me as "slim fine" back then. While hanging out on Bourbon, we meet these three guys and started talking to them. When we were ready to head home and told them we were leaving, they asked us if we needed a ride home. This was in the '90s, so we were used to getting in the car with strangers. Hell, it wasn't the first time we just jumped into someone's car. Also, one man from the group was trying to get with Keedy. The first stop we made was by my great-grandmother's house uptown, where I had hidden my clothes in the apartment laundromat. I had placed them there because I planned to stay at Keedy's house that night. I grabbed my clothes and returned to the car. One guy stated, "Hey, do ya'll want to chill with us for a bit before ya'll leave us?" Keedy looked at me and replied, "Yeah." In the back of my mind, that little feeling came back again. This would be the first of many times I ignored it. I simply responded, "Okay."

As they pulled off, we started heading into the section of New Orleans called Gert Town. I had been familiar with the area because it was near where my aunt used to live. We pull up to a house and got out of the car. The guys were like, "Ya'll come inside and chill.

We got drinks." I pulled Keedy to the side and told her, "Something is not right about these guys, and we need to go." Keedy was like, "Girl, you are tripping—they mad cool. Everything is okay." And, yet again, I got that feeling, and it was worse than ever.

I felt nervous, anxious, and my stomach was in knots. Keedy went into the house first, with two of the guys. I was still standing outside, and the third guy and I went to take a walk around the neighborhood. We walked and talked for about fifteen minutes, getting to know each other. When we made it back to the house, he expressed that we should go inside to get my friend. I complied and opened the front door, not bothering to knock.

As we walked into the house, I could tell that he had kids. The space was filled with toys and kids' clothing. Stuff was just everywhere. It looked as if the people that lived there never cleaned their home. As I waited in the living room for Keedy to come from the back of the house, I put my head down, thinking, *Why it is taking her so long?* As I lifted my head back up, one man walked into the living room bottomless and holding a gun in his hand. Then he put the gun to my face. In my mind, I was like, *Oh shit! What have I gotten myself into?* The dude looked into my eyes and told me, "If you do what I say, I will let you live." As the men pulled me to the back of the house, I yelled, "Where is my friend?" One man turned around and yelled, "That bitch is already giving that pussy up and now it's your turn." I burst into tears, thinking to myself, *Lord help me get out of this.* I did not want to have my virginity taken like this, or die.

As I was being forced down the hallway, I noticed Keedy sitting on top of a washer in the laundry room, having sex with one of the three men. It almost looked as if she was enjoying it. They shoved me into a bathroom. Next, one of them pulled my pants down. I started shouting that I was only thirteen years old. One guy yelled, "You wanted to be grown, so I'm going to show you how to be grown." In that moment I nearly blacked out as, one by one, each of them took their turn. I had always grown up in the church but never prayed or understood it. But that night, I prayed like I had never prayed before.

After they finished, they forced me to open my mouth while they each ejaculated into it. All I could feel was the severe pain all over my body. Afterward, one man dragged me by my hair out of the bathroom and back into the living room, where Keedy was being held by another man. The men were talking to each other, trying to figure out what should they do with us. One yelled, "Dude, we got to get rid of them! I will not go to jail over this!" Seeing the man panic over what they had just done, I mumbled, "If you let us go, we won't say nothing or tell anyone." He ordered the other two men to grab some pillowcases and place them over our heads. Then they led us into their car while pressing a gun against the back of our heads. The time in the car felt like an eternity. The car suddenly stopped, and we got thrown onto what felt like grass. They pulled the pillowcases off our heads and one of them told us, "If you turn around or tell anyone, we will find you and kill you."

As we lay on the ground, we could hear the screeching sound of car tires peeling off. I counted to ten in my head, then slowly turned around to peek, to see if they had left. They had. We jumped up and ran until we saw a police car parked in a distance. As we got closer to the parked police car, we could hear another car approaching us. I feared that the men had come back to kill us. I quickly grabbed Keedy, and we hid between cars parked nearby until we heard it pass.

Just when we began walking toward the police car, we saw a man jump out of a car and run in our direction. The closer he got, I noticed it was a man from the group. I wasn't sure if the guilt or regret of what they had done kicked in or if it was his way of luring us back so they could kill us. Once in front of us, though, he started apologizing. Then he offered to bring us home. Keedy's dumb ass looked at me as if she was considering it. I gave her the harshest look I could give, then ran to the police car, and she followed me. Once we got the officer's attention, he told us to get in his car. I looked back to see if the man's car was still behind us, but it had disappeared. I explained to the officer what had taken place. I noticed that Keedy was quiet the entire time. The officer listened and explained to us that he needed to get us to the nearest hospital, then he contacted detectives from his unit.

As I lay on a hospital exam room table, I felt the same feeling that I had felt after being molested: *Why me?* Then there was a knock on the door. It was a doctor and nurse coming into the room to examine me. The nurse pulled out a rape kit and assisted the doctor with checking me from head to toe. They took pictures, gave me a host of medications, performed a pelvic exam, and tried to collect any DNA they could from my body. I just closed my eyes and checked out of reality.

Afterward, they escorted us to the police station, where they contacted my mom. Since I was a minor, they could not talk to me until she was present. I had pleaded with the officers not to contact her, but to no avail. My mother arrived as the officer placed Keedy and me into two separate rooms.

As my mother and I sat in the room waiting, she did not utter a word. She didn't ask me how I was feeling or what had happened. She didn't ask me anything. Two detectives—a middle-aged black woman and an older man—entered the room and notified us that they were being assigned to our case. During the interview, they asked me several questions. As I explained what had happened, they both looked as if I disgusted them. When I was finished, the lady stated that I was lying and she thought I just had sex with those men. Next thing I knew, all hell broke loose in that office. I snapped, cussing their asses out from A to Z. It did not dawn on me that my mom was sitting right next to me. Once I settled down, their expressions changed. The female detective told me to calm down. They looked at each other, then she looked at me and said, "We had to be sure who was telling the truth. I was like, "What?" The detectives informed me that Keedy's story didn't match the story that I was telling them. This led them to believe that one of us was lying. I snapped back, "I am not lying, and I can take ya'll to the house where it happened. "They looked at each other again and the male detective said, "OK, show us." We left the precinct and got into an unmarked police car. As they drove, I remembered every turn we took. Before I knew it, we were in front of the exact house. The detectives took notes, and we returned to the station. Back at the station, the detectives must have run some sort of search on their computers because they were able to find out who the owners of the house were. I also provided them with a full description of the layout of the house and all items in it, down to the children's toys. Before leaving the station, the female detective's last words to me were, "Keedy is not your friend, and if I were you, I would stop hanging with her."

Those words stuck in my head. Back at my mother's house, three days after the attack, I sank into deep depression and a lost sense of reality. That Sunday, I tried going back to church with my mother to seek clarity, but after sitting there for an hour, I could overhear my mother telling the older ladies what had happened to me. Some stuff she mentioned wasn't even true. After I caught her gossiping with these so-called Christians, in walked the same two detectives from the police station. I thought to myself, *They came into the Lord's house with this foolishness.* We went into a room at the back of the church, where they pulled out pictures and wanted me to point out the men who harmed me. When I saw their faces in the lineup of photos, I explained the role each one played while they took down more of my statement. As they were leaving, the detectives explained to me that Keedy lied, and they found her to be a willing participant. Worse, she knowingly put me in that situation. Learning that information left me in total disbelief. It all came together, why she was acting the way she did. I left the church and got on my hood shit and called my aunts. One of them began helping me plot to beat the shit out of her. We had it all planned out. My aunt would talk her into coming to her house so I could whoop her ass. The plan was in motion, and we waited for her. I mean, I was in the house practicing like a boxer getting ready for the ring. But she never showed up.

After this storm, I spent several months searching for her. Later, I found out she had moved to Texas. Oh, but when the day comes . . . I don't give a damn how old I am, I'm still going to whip her ass. As for the rapists, they were arrested, and a court day was soon approaching. However, somehow one of the men was able to track me down and started harassing me. I contacted the police, however the only witness protection they offered was to move to the next parish which was across the street. I was so terrified I just told the officers since I was still a minor I didn't want to testify or see them ever again in life. That would be the last time I hear from the officers regarding my rape.

Chapter Three

Recovery

*A*few weeks had passed since the rape, and I discovered myself being paranoid, terrified, and bitter. It looked as if l was living in a world where there wasn't anybody I could turn to. Not even family. Everyone around me just acted as if nothing happened. My psychological state was one dominated by suicidal thoughts. I no longer cared about my life and felt like whatever happened would happen; it was what it was. Besides having suicidal thoughts, I became exasperated with any- and everyone. One day, as I was cleaning up, I found my hospital papers and noticed that the nurse gave me a referral to a local YMCA, with a brief note attached: "If you ever needed someone to talk to, call Ms. Jackson."

I sat and debated my choices awhile, questioning, *Should I call this lady? What help could she offer?* I decided not to call out of the fear of being judged. So I chose to keep all my feelings to myself. Living with my mother again, I was ready to get back to high school and try to figure this thing called life out.

Because of my reckless behavior in previous schools, I had to enroll in an alternative school for a year as a punishment. However, the joke was on the courts because I found it to be entertaining and enlightening. Starting my ninth-grade school year was okay, but I was still suffering from the trauma I experienced. My paranoia had gotten worse, and I was looking over my shoulder at every turn. I carried a butcher knife in my book bag and razor blades under my tongue at all times. As I sat in class one day, I thought about the note the nurse had left for me and made the call to seek help when I got home that afternoon. I had grown tired and weary.

I arrived at the facility and asked for Ms. Jackson. She was an older, short lady that looked like someone's grandmother. As I introduced myself to her, she just uttered, "I know who you are." We walked down the hallway and into a small room. As I entered the room, there was a group of girls sitting in a circle staring at me as if they were thinking, *About time she made it.* The first session lasted an hour. Within that hour-long session, I discovered there were others like me. The young ladies shared their stories of uncles, dads, brothers, and other men raping them. Listening to their stories gave me a fresh perspective. One girl told her story about being raped by her mother's boyfriend for years. When she told her mom, her mother didn't believe her. She repeated the old quote that is used far too often in the African American community: "What happens in this house stays in this house." It wasn't until she went to the hospital and learned she was pregnant with his child that she escaped the torture.

As I continued to listen, I couldn't help but notice that the way she told her story was as if it was nothing. Once finished, she turned to me and asked what my story was. However, I was too ashamed, so I just answered that I wasn't ready to tell. After the session was over, I asked Ms. Jackson how she could manage hearing these horrible stories. She laughed, then answered, "It's not about me. Everyone needs an outlet, someone they can relate to, and somewhere to feel safe without judgement. I was once in your shoes too." Those words to me triggered something that I had never felt. *Hope.* From that day on, I went to the sessions twice a week. I attended them for three months, just listening to everyone. After three months, my twelve sessions were complete. Even though I was still filled with so much shame and embarrassment, I never told my story or how my rapist was able to get away with it, and they never forced me.

As time went on, I found my own way of coping with what happened. Looking at my situation, I don't think anyone can ever say they fully recover from being a victim of rape and molestation. You just suppress it or develop certain personality traits from it. In the aftermath of that night, I made the choice to stop hanging in the streets and concentrate on school.

The next year, I returned to a public school to finish my last three years of high school and found the perfect outlet to stay out of trouble: I joined my high school band. Being in the band made me feel like I had a real family. It was structured, discipline, and we were always there for each other. My bandmates were my support system. Although school seemed to go great, my home life was a different story.

I still didn't live with my mom. To best explain, my home life was me jumping from house to house, living with all my aunts, my great-grandmother, or anyone that would let me spend the night. It was not because I preferred to be living from pillar to post, but more of my mother making me feel unwanted. Most of the time, I ended up staying with my great-grandmother

Dorothy. My great-grandmother and I were close. She was a character. The best way to describe her is to compare her to Tyler Perry's Madea character. She would tell you some out-of-this-world shit and dare you to say something about it. Yes, a real ole-school type, with whom you knew what she wanted you to do just by the way she stared at you. She never sugarcoated anything and gave it to you raw, dry, and uncut. It didn't matter how old you were. She always talked about people and life. She would tell me stuff and I would just nod my head and pretend to understand. However, she was someone I could confide in. I disclosed to her what happened, and she was speechless. She pulled out the little gun she kept in her purse and asked me to show her where my attackers lived. Of course, I had to pretend I didn't know, otherwise she would have done something to them. When she calmed down, her words were, "Everyone has been though something, baby— it's called life. If you don't get ahold of it now, it will screw you up later. Also, not everybody is your friend. People are leaves; they change on you. Give it time. You need to know the difference in the structure of your tree so you can know what to expect and won't confuse them with roots." I told her, "Yes, ma'am," just so she would stop preaching and asking me questions.

Years passed; I was now a senior in high school and thriving. I was happy to be finally graduating. Joining the school band had paid off. With the guidance from our band directors, I was offered a partial college scholarship to the amazing J State (a.k.a. Jackson State, to be exact). Receiving the letter from the school made me feel a sense of achievement. However, just as quickly as it excited me, boom, my reality hit me. I did not have a way to pay for school, even with a scholarship. The only thing left for me to do was to tuck my tail between my legs and swallow my fears and asked my mother to help pay for college.

Later that night, I stopped by my mother's house and asked. Just as quickly as I asked, she responded, in one breath, with, "Nope. I am not taking out any loans for my children. You better figure it out on your own." Her response didn't make me angry, but it made me feel sorry for her. As I processed her words, I just chalked it up to her own challenges and thought to myself, *When I have kids, I will never treat them that way.*

The next day, I started weighing my other options and looking at what I had going for myself. One thing

I knew was that I did not want to be a product of my environment. My mindset was focused on growth and not allowing my life to be a part of a societal norm that too many people fall victim to in New Orleans—the lack of an education. Then it hit me! I could go into the military.

I could have them pay for college and have a job. This would be like a two-for-one special. The next day, I contacted a recruiter and began the process. The recruiter sent me to take the ASVAB exam, which I completed successfully.

After receiving my scores which were high enough for enlistment, my recruiter scheduled me to take the physical at a place they called the MEPs office. If you ever thought about enlisting, this was the office where you got sent for a physical, to pick a job, and to get sworn in.

Later that night, the recruiter dropped me off at the hotel with other recruits, to spend the night and take the physical in the morning. What he failed to tell me was that I would share a room with a stranger. They put me in with a girl that was so weird I had to sleep with one eye open. It was as if she had never met a black girl before. She asked questions about my hair and why I talked the way I did. It seemed as if she had assumed I couldn't speak proper English. I thought to myself, *I know she is fucking lying.* Then I whispered under my breath, "If I survived the projects, I can survive one night with this bitch."

The next morning, we left to go to the MEPs office for the physical. I will say this: I never had a physical like this before. These people had me doing things I never even heard of, such as duck walking. What in the hell was *that*? To top it off, I was in the room with several other women recruits. When I looked around, all I could hear in my head was my grandmother saying, *Always make sure you have clean and cute underwear.* You never know what's going to happen." So many females had holes in their underwear and raggedy-ass bras. I felt sorry for them. I know it embarrassed them. Once I finished, I was like, *Thank you, Jesus.* The only thing left to do was to wait one month until my eighteenth birthday so I could swear in and not worry about parental consent. I just knew I was on my way to make something of myself . . . or so I thought.

Chapter Four

I bet you all thought I made it and enlisted, huh? Well, I hate to break it to you . . . life threw me a curveball. That curveball was a man named Thomas. My grandmother always told us, "A man will make you lose focus on your dreams." She was right. Meeting this man changed my entire world.

It was my eighteenth birthday. Time to turn up and get loose as a goose. Since I was of legal age, what better way to celebrate than to go to a 50-cent concert. I got all dressed up in the skimpiest dress that revealed all my little curves. I didn't have a car, so I had to ride public transportation to get around the city. After getting dolled up, I headed out to the nearest bus stop. While waiting for the bus, a man pulled in blasting music you could hear a mile away. He jumped out of the car, and, for a moment, our eyes locked on each other. Not trying to be noticeable, I played it off as if I hadn't seen him, but looking out of my peripheral vision, I could see him walking toward me. Then I heard, "Excuse me, miss, can I have a second of your time to talk to you?"

Of course, I played hard to get, replying, "All you get is a second. I have somewhere to go." In the back of my head, I was like, *Hell yeah, you can talk to me.* This man was just a little taller than me, dark, handsome, smelled good, and had perfect teeth.

We started conversing, and it was very intriguing, almost as if we already knew each other. As our conservation grew more intense, I could hear the bus approaching. So I cut the conversation off and was like, "My bus is here and I have somewhere to be." He looked puzzled and stuttered, "W-where are you going? I'll give you a ride." I got into his car and we drove around, talking so much I missed the concert. He felt bad for making me miss the show and offered to reimburse me for the cost of the ticket. I looked at my watch and just told him he could drop me off at home.

We pulled up to my apartment, and he offered to walk me to my door. It looked as if he wanted me to invite him in for a nightcap, but I just thanked him and told him I'll call tomorrow. Over the next month, we saw each other every day. The chemistry between us was profound. He seemed to care about me.

After one of our dates, I invited him into my apartment. I offered him something to drink and, before I could hand him the glass, we were all over each other, and all over the house. I would say this man gave me what I like to call an all-night special. I didn't even know a person could go that long. The next morning, we had breakfast, and he went his way and I went mine. I started contemplating and compartmentalizing what had just happened between us. I knew I was trying to enlist in the US Navy and be on my way. I didn't want to be in a serious relationship, so I made up my mind to play with this dude until it was time for me to leave. After that, I would never see him again. Yep, that could work.

However, the more we saw each other, the more feelings grew. Also, the more feelings grew, the more reckless I became. We saw each other every day and had sex each time. One day, in the middle of having sex, the condom broke. We both jumped up, and I ran into the bathroom, trying an asinine method of pushing out whatever sperm may have gotten inside me. I cleaned myself up and walked out the bathroom. He looked nervously at me and asked, "Did you get it all out?" (I guess that makes him dummy number two.) "Yeah, I think so," I said.

Another month passed, and it was time for me to go back to the MEPs office with my US Navy recruiter to swear in. He advised that it had been a minute since the last time I was there, and they wanted me to take a pregnancy test before we completed everything. I wasn't sure if this was the normal procedure, but I was like, okay, whatever. I took the urine test, and it came back positive. When that recruiter said, "Um, Keisha, you are pregnant, and we can't move forward with your enlistment," my heart sank and my expression froze—I couldn't speak. Only thing on my mind was, *Fuck!*

I arrived home and called Thomas to tell him I was pregnant. We talked about abortion as an option but decided to go through with my pregnancy. He assured me everything was going to be okay and this might be a blessing. We also discussed our ability to afford a baby. He answered, "I'm a hustler. I can make some sells to get us whatever we need." This gave me a sense of comfort since it was normal in my circles to have a baby daddy that sold drugs.

Being around Thomas during my pregnancy, I started noticing his personality flaws. It was as if his representative had left and he was now showing who he really was. The first thing I noticed was that he never came, or wanted to come, to any of my doctor's appointments with me. I thought this was rather odd since this was the first kid for both of us. You would think he would want to hear the first heartbeat or see the first ultrasound. Every time I asked why he didn't want to come; he would just utter he that he didn't like doctors or hospitals since his mom passed away in one of them. His response made me feel alone and abandoned. However, I found a justifiable reason for his reaction in my head and put his feelings first, rather than my own. I never asked him again.

As it came time to break the news about the pregnancy, I took him to meet my mom as his introduction to my family. When my mom saw him, she pulled me to the side and told me she knew him already. I was like, *okay*, but then she told me he was dating one of her coworkers. She rolled her eyes, crossed her arms, then told me Thomas "ain't no good" and I needed to leave him. Of course, I became defensive and told her she didn't know what she was talking about and I wasn't trying to take her seriously.

After leaving my mother's house, I confronted Thomas with the comments my mother had made. He denied everything. He confessed they had dated, but it had been over for a while. Listening to him gave me a feeling that he was not telling the truth. But I couldn't argue since I had become dependent on him to take care of me. I dropped the subject and moved on. The following week, we moved into a tiny one-bedroom apartment. It felt like a fresh start. This was going to be our happily ever after, like what you see on TV or in Hallmark movies. However, this would be the beginning of the storm.

Chapter Five

The Storm

I was finally in my own apartment. No more living by anyone one else's rules! It was just Thomas and me starting our life together. We got what little we owned set up in the house. As we settled in for the night, I realized this was the first time I had ever lived with a man. I didn't know what to expect or what I should do, so I did what came naturally and started decorating to make the apartment feel homey.

When I finished decorating, I started hanging our clothes in the closet; however, I could see Thomas acting strange out of the corners of my eyes. He sat drinking whiskey and rambling about something and I had no clue what he was saying. I thought maybe it was the liquor talking. I walked into our closet and heard the door shutting behind me. I spun around, walked to door, and turned the handle to open it. He had locked it. Not being a fan of being in small, confined places, I panicked. I banged on the door and screamed to get Thomas's attention. All I could hear was him laughing. It wasn't a normal-person laugh, but more of an evil, snickering laughter. Then he then yelled, "If you want to get out you have to do everything I tell you to do when I say do it." At first, I thought he was joking. I started cursing and kept yelling at him to just "open the damn door." However, he just yelled back, "Not until you agree!" At that moment, I felt powerless and afraid, as I had when I was a little girl being molested and, later, assaulted. As I continued to weep and beg him to let me out, he continued to refuse. After fifteen minutes had passed, I gave in and agreed to his terms. Then he opened the door.

I asked him why he would do something like that. He smiled and then replied that he was just playing. Something in me gave me the feeling that he wasn't playing, and this was a warning sign of what would come next. I was pregnant and didn't have anywhere to run to, so I shrugged it off and stayed.

As my belly grew bigger and bigger, I noticed Thomas drinking more and even sleeping out or coming home in the wee hours of the night. I would ask him where he was and all I would get from him was, "Oh, I was drinking and fell asleep at a friend's house," or, "I fell asleep at a bus station." In my heart I knew it was a lie, but our son was on the way. I wanted him to have something I never had: a family with both parents in the home. One day, I asked him if he could help me put our son's baby crib together. My stomach was enormous, plus using tools was not my strong suit. Thomas just looked at me and uttered, "Nope. You wanted it, you put it together."

With the hormones raging in my body, that ghetto girl came out of me. I snapped and told him, "Well, I'll be damned. You got me fucked up if you think I am putting together this bed with your ass sitting here drinking. It's bad enough you don't come to any of my doctor's appointments." Now the argument was on. "I do whatever the hell I feel like!" he yelled and walked toward the front door. I jumped in front of him and asked, again, "So you're not going to help me?" Within seconds, almost like a reflex, Thomas grabbed me by the neck, slammed me against the wall, and began choking me. All I could hear was the sound of his voice yelling, "Bitch, I said leave me alone!" Once he stopped, I ran into the room and burst into tears. I cried, as this was the first time he had physically harmed me. I didn't know what to do. In my environment, this was what they called love. I let him leave, wiped away my tears, and put the baby crib together myself.

He's here! My baby boy, Jacob, arrived, seven pounds, five point nine ounces of perfection. There is nothing more special than seeing your child for the first time. I would say childbirth is beautiful, but that would be a lie. My son almost killed me! Childbirth pain is the worst pain *ever*! Thomas swallowed his pride and joined me in the delivery room. Having him by my side was quite awkward. When my doctor met him, he whispered to me, "Girl, I thought your baby daddy didn't exist." I just looked at him and smiled in order to not expose my embarrassment.

After staying in the hospital for two days, they discharged me and Jacob, and we were free to go home. Thank God my mother was at the hospital with us during my stay. I didn't know what to do with an infant. She even rode home with us to make sure the house was cleaned and setup for Jacob.

We entered the house to get settled in, and I was still in awe of this little baby I was now responsible for. To my surprise, my mom's attitude changed, and she seemed to be helpful and caring. I thought little of it, and as a new mom, you need all the help you can get. However, the new baby did not change Thomas's behavior. It was like living with Dr. Jekyll and Mr.

Hyde. He would be nice one day and hateful the next day. This was our routine. I know you may wonder why I stayed with him. It's because he was a broken soul I thought I could fix. Thomas grew up in circumstances similar to mine. His mom was a single mother who also fell victim to a drug addiction. I thought to myself that if I just loved him a little more or tried a little harder to do things the way he wanted, it would make everything right.

A year passed, and I found that being a young mother made you consider what was important in life. Since meeting Thomas and having Jacob, I forgot about my dream of going into the military. Now it was time to think about plan B. I loved helping and taking care of people, so the next best thing would be to look into becoming a nurse. When I mentioned it to Thomas, his response was, "You have to be smart to do that, and you need to find a babysitter." I walked away and mumbled, "Whatever," under my breath.

The next day, with nursing school on my mind, I sat down and created a plan. Since I wasn't working and relied on Thomas for everything, I had to figure out a way to pay for school. *Bam!* It hit me. I thought to myself, I can enroll in a technical college first, get some skills, along with childcare, then transfer to a community college.

By fall, I enrolled in a local technical college and was on my way.

I completed school and left as a certified nursing assistant, along with being a medical assistant. Next steps were to get a job and transfer to a community college nursing program. Although the situation at home wasn't the best, I tuned Thomas out and continued pushing forward. Unfortunately, like they say, when things are going well, something always comes along to fuck it up. This time, it was Hurricane Katrina.

August 29, 2005, is a day I will never forget. This storm hit New Orleans as if God was mad at the city. We lost everything. When I say everything, we were homeless. At the time, Thomas had been working on a cruise boat, so it was just Jacob and me. Given the size of the storm, I packed as many of my things as I could in my car and headed to Houston, Texas, where my oldest sister, Carla, offered us a safe haven.

My sister and I were a couple of years apart and we barely talked, maybe once a year. However, she was nice enough to allow my son and me to stay with her. I was very grateful that she offered. Sometimes that so-called kindness has a way of revealing the ugly truth about a person, though. As we were on our way to her apartment, she mentioned that our other family members would be there, and we would have to get in where we fit in. I thought that maybe this would give us a chance to get to know one another. Chile, whoever said blood is thicker than water, is full of shit.

After staying with my sister for three days, I realized how cutthroat people can be. Soon she asked me to leave her house after I refused to allow another family member to sleep on my air mattress while my son and I slept on the floor. I didn't argue or pick a fight, because this was her house and those were the rules she wanted me to follow. I wasn't with it, so I packed up my stuff and left to find the nearest hotel. Later, Thomas joined us. I explained what had occurred and told him I thought it would be best to leave Houston and head to Atlanta, Georgia. The next day, we packed everything into the car and we were on our way.

As we arrived in Atlanta, it amazed me to see this city. Never had I been to a place where there were so many successful black people. Living in New Orleans, most people were a product of their environment. You never saw black entrepreneurship or millionaires. It felt as if I was where I belonged. We found a hotel in a town called Buckhead where they were letting Katrina victims stay for free. As we toured the area, we couldn't help but notice so many people offering us help. Thomas didn't fall in love with the city, so he would always remind me not to get happy living in Atlanta. He made sure I understood that as soon as New Orleans opened back up, we were returning.

Whelp, that time came, and I-10 reopened, so we left Atlanta, heading back to New Orleans. When we arrived home, there wasn't anything to come back to. Our apartment had sustained significant damage. Our only option for a place to stay was a FEMA trailer in front of his aunt's home for $200 a month. We were thankful and made the best out of a horrible situation.

Luckily, few people came back to the city, so I could find a job quickly and get back to school. The job was rather interesting. I was a manager of a mansion-turned-guesthouse in the French Quarter. My relationship with Thomas became strained. When he realized I was back in school and working, he would do spiteful things, such as leave before it was time for me to go to work and then tell me I needed to find a babysitter. Another thing he would do is not pick our son up from day care, knowing I didn't get off in time to get him. Frustrated, I would seek guidance from women I knew. They would tell me that, hell, if he was paying the bills, I should just let him be. That's what I did. Though we were struggling to get along, I found out I was pregnant again.

I wasn't sad at the thought of being pregnant again, but I soon would be. As I contemplated how to tell Thomas, he arrived at the house with a bottle of whiskey, looking as if he had lost his best friend. As he sat pouring a drink, I blurted, "I have something to tell you." He added, "I have something to tell you too." The next words out of my mouth were, "I'm pregnant." His response was, "Well, I have two kids on the way now." I was like, "What? What did you just say?" He simply stated, "I have another woman pregnant too."

My heart just sank. It was like a piercing in my chest, and the tears just came rolling down my face. The only word that came out of my mouth was, "Why?" He gave excuses being drunk one night, and said it was something that just happened. I was numb, confused, scared, and bitter all at the same time. Not only was this the man I had tolerated a lot of shit from, but I was in love with him. My internal reaction to him was, *Not only did you cheat on me, but you had unprotected sex with this person and could have brought something home to me.* I just walked away. As I lay in the bed, I felt as if I had done something wrong and analyzed myself to see what made him seek other women.

Later that night, I fell asleep lying in the bed with my son. I was awakened by a sharp pain spreading from my right eye. I opened my eyes, and Thomas was on top of me, screaming, "Why are you playing with me?" The force of his hand hitting my face was so strong, it stung. Instead of fighting back, I pushed my son Jacob into the closet and closed the door so he could not witness his mother being beaten. The attack went on for about five minutes until his sister, who was at the house at the time, heard me screaming for him to stop. She dragged him from the room. Once he left, I curled up in my bed next to my son, not knowing what to do. There wasn't any family to call as I realized he had isolated me from them. I didn't know who to run to for help.

The next morning, I got dressed for work and noticed that my face was swollen, I had a black eye, and there were bruises all over my body. As I dressed my son for day care, he asked, "Mommy, Daddy hit you in the eye?" While ashamed, I told him, "No, baby, we were just wrestling." After dropping him off at day care,

I went to the nearest store to buy concealer to cover my eye. I tried my hardest to cover my face with the makeup in hopes my coworkers didn't notice, but they did. Alisha, who was the assistant manager, pulled me to the side and said, "We see you with a black eye and you can't hide it. If you are with someone that is beating you, that is not love and you need to leave them before they kill you." Although her words rang true, I became defensive. I asked her to mind the business that pays her. She just replied, "I'm here for you if you need me."

The day went on and she said nothing else about it. After work, I picked my son up from day care and made the long drive home. When I arrived at the house, I just sat in the car, contemplating what I should do next. I got out of the car and went inside, not knowing what was in store. When I walked in, I could see Thomas standing in the kitchen, cooking. There were flowers on the counter. When he saw me, he apologized for what he had done and begged me not to leave him. He promised he would slow down with drinking and even suggested we move to an unfamiliar state, such as Virginia, so we could have a fresh start.

It was pretty talk, but somehow, I knew he wasn't capable of such big changes. I accepted his apology and decided to give him another chance.

Chapter Six

Survival

As you all would imagine, I took him back and tried to make my little family work. Within a few months, we moved from New Orleans to Staunton, Virginia. It was going to be a fresh start and we would leave all the bullshit behind. Virginia wasn't exactly a random location; it was also where my father lived. Maybe this would give me an opportunity to get to know him.

Staunton, Virginia, was a beautiful city surrounded by mountains, with breathtaking views. I had never been up north before, and I was just in awe. The trees were enormous and covered in reddish orange leaves. The air was clear and crisp to the point that New Orleans was the last thing on my mind. Prior to leaving New Orleans, we signed a lease on a nice townhome in Staunton. Later that night, once we had arrived and settled in, we met up with my dad, Frank. He gave us a tour around the city and even showed me some places where I could find work.

Within two weeks of arriving, I enrolled my son in day care and started working in a local nursing home on weekends as a med tech and at the nearest hospital as a nursing assistant on weekdays. Thomas wasn't working at the time, so I became the breadwinner. Even though we hadn't been in the city long, his old habits came right back. He spent his days drinking and nights going out to local hangouts. I thought to myself, *Here we go again.* We had not been here six months, and he reverted to the same ole Thomas.

Time passed, and I was in my third trimester with our second baby. Things had not gotten better. Thomas reverted to a full-blown alcoholic. It was as if mentally I was in a sunken place. I would often sleep in my son's room just to escape him. I felt like a prisoner in my home. If I would mention anything about his behavior, he would rant about my appearance and the growing size of my belly. He also would say that no one would ever love me the way he did. The weirdest thing was, the next day, he would say he didn't remember telling me anything. He would just come in the room excited, as if nothing had ever happened.

Well, one time, just like on any other day, he came next to me looking excited about something. I asked him what happened this time. He told me that the woman he got pregnant had given birth to their baby girl. Reality hit me like a gut punch, that this man was the father of another child, who was not ours. The only word that came out my mouth was, "Congratulations," as I turned and walked away. I retreated to my room and all I could do was cry. After a while, I convinced myself that if I stayed with this man, I would have to take whatever came with him. Child and baby mama included.

Later that night, I asked him if I could meet the mama and baby. He looked at me and said, "No. For what?" I mentioned that if I was going to accept the situation, I would like the meet them. He gave me this evil stare and just walked away. Later on that night, he came back in the room and said he wanted to tell me something. In my mind I was like, *Here we go*, and braced myself for whatever came out of his mouth. Then he said the words, "I don't love you no more, and I found someone else." I had no emotion to show. It was as if I already knew. He told me about the woman as though she had everything that I didn't. Then he pulled up her picture from his phone to show me. I just responded, "Okay."

In the morning, I woke up before Thomas. Looking over at him in the bed, I just felt rage. I wanted him to feel the same pain I had been feeling for years. Without thinking, I grabbed a pillow and covered his face and attempted to smother him. As I had the pillow over his face, I could hear a little voice saying, *Don't do it, he's not worth it.* I removed the pillow from his face and let him go free, and he jumped up and left without saying one word to me.

He left for a week. Not having him around was the best feeling ever. However, I was nine months pregnant and due any day, so I still felt as if I needed him. When he finally came back to the house, he said nothing, and neither did I. We acted as if we were just roommates.

Two days later, I went into labor while waiting for my appointment at the doctor's office. I called Thomas and told him I needed him to bring me to the hospital, but he just told me to drive myself. Of course, his response pissed me off, but I didn't have time to argue. I left the clinic and drove myself to the hospital. Once I settled in my room, I called Thomas again just to see if he was coming to see our son being born. Shockingly, he said yes.

Hours passed, but he still hadn't arrived. My midwife entered the room to perform a check and informed me it was time to push. I called Thomas again, and he said he was on his way. What Thomas didn't know was that

I added a locator to his cell phone that showed his exact location, courtesy of Alltel phone services. I looked at the locator and noticed he was at some apartments that weren't anywhere near the hospital. It pissed me off. *This man is with his bitch while I am in labor*, I thought. Thirty more minutes passed, and he showed up as I started pushing.

After being discharged from the hospital, I arrived home and my house was a disaster. It looked as if no one had cleaned it in days. Thomas drove away after dropping me off and I tried calling him over and over, but my calls went unanswered. I was beyond angry at this point. I used the locator app again to pinpoint his location, packed my kids in the car, and went on a mission to hunt him down. *No more will I be the fool.* I spotted his car parked outside some apartments. Pulling up, I sent him a message to come outside. After five minutes, he came down the stairs yelling, "Why are you here? I told you I don't want you!" I told him everything that was on my mind and cursed him out from A to Z. I felt as if I had finally found my courage and was no longer afraid. As we continued to argue, he saw I wasn't backing down. He turned around and walked away, slinking back into the woman's apartment.

Still in my fit of rage, I called Thomas's phone and told him to come back outside. He just hung up on me. That was the last straw. I saw the car he cherished so much and took my anger out on it. He needed to feel as much, if not more, pain that I had felt from being with him. I began slashing his tires and busting his windows. Then I called him back and told him what I did. In true brute nature, he came running outside, ready to fight. This time, I was ready to go toe to toe. I would love to say I won the fight, but the truth is, I didn't. He knocked me to the ground and choked me to the point that I passed out. It felt like an out-of-body experience and I was staring at myself on the ground. It was as if something was showing me that this was not the last memory I wanted my kids to have of me. I came to and drove my kids and myself back home. Since no one was outside to witness the fight, I decided not to call the police in fearing that I would be the one to go to jail since I drove over there to him. After cleaning myself up from the fight, I sent him a text message to come get all his stuff and leave. Nothing mattered anymore. It didn't matter that I was not working at the time and didn't have any money to pay the bills or that I was facing eviction.

A week passed, and eviction letter came in the mail. I didn't know what to do. For so many years, I depended on this man for everything. I didn't know where the kids and I would go or how we were going to survive. I tucked my tail between my legs and called Thomas. When he answered, I swallowed my pride and asked if he could help me pay the bills so I could keep a roof over our children's heads until they cleared me to go back to work. He laughed and said, "No. You wanted me gone, you got it. Now you need to figure it out on your own."

All I thought was, *Wow*. I didn't have time to dwell on the moment for too long. It was time for me to see if I could find any government or community programs that could help. I found one, but the lady at the center told me I had to be at the center at eight o'clock in the morning and to get there early because the lines got long and they only accepted so many people.

The next morning, I packed my kids up in the car and made sure I was the first in line. We arrived there around four o'clock that morning and parked right in front of the door. After waiting hours were over, they started letting everyone in. I filled out the application and they ushered me in a room with a caseworker. She reviewed my application and told me I didn't qualify for any help since I still had a few days in my apartment left. I explained to the lady that it was only a matter of days till my two children and I became homeless. She just looked me in the face and said, "Sorry, there isn't anything I can do." I grabbed all my paperwork, thanked her for her time, gathered my kids, and left.

I made it back to my apartment and started going through everything to determine what I could fit in my car and what I had to get rid of. In doing so, I burst into tears. My tears were from the sorrow of facing my kids and realizing I couldn't even provide the simplest thing for them: a home. While alone with my thoughts, I felt a little tap on my shoulder. It was my son Jacob saying, "Mommy, it's going to be okay." I turned to him and said, "You are right—it will be." I got up from the floor, called my doctor, explained my situation, and got a clearance to return to work just over a week after giving birth. By the end of the week, I was homeless but happy.

After getting approved for childcare assistance at no cost, I went back to work. Since we didn't have a place to live, I would park my car in the hospital parking lot to have somewhere safe to sleep. In the mornings, we would just go to the restroom through the hospital's emergency room to wash off and clean up. I don't think anyone noticed us since I wore my scrub uniform. It was as if we blended in. When I received my first check, I took my money and paid for stays at a nearby motel. But I knew living in a motel was still considered homeless and not something I wanted to continue. I decided it was in my best interest to move us back to New Orleans. Over the next three months, I saved up enough money, packed up the kids, and headed home.

Chapter Seven

Twilight Zone

oving back home was not only the hardest decision to make but I felt like such a failure. After so many years of being on my own, it was a tough pill to swallow, moving back into my mother's house. Even though I looked okay on the outside, on the inside, I was suffering. Being in an abusive relationship made me feel as if I had lost my voice. As if I couldn't survive without him. Maybe it was Stockholm syndrome. Shortly after our arrival, Thomas came knocking. Unbeknownst to me, he returned to New Orleans to look for a new job shortly before I did. Once again, I fell to weakness and fear. Thomas was back in our lives.

He convinced me we needed to be together for the sake of our kids. To give them a life that neither one of us experienced, with both parents being together. Like always, though, the sweet, caring, gentle representative left and his true colors revealed themselves. This time, I had no energy left to fight. He had me trained and programmed. My daily living was just existing. With each mirror I would walk in front of, I could not recognize the person who stood there. He conditioned me to buy into his idea of what I should be and how I should act. He broke me. . . . There were times I avoided speaking to people of the opposite sex for fear that he would find out and it would lead to a fight. My life had become an endless routine of nightmares.

Through the cycle, I'd given birth to our third son. Looking at my children triggered something within me. The final straw came after visiting Thomas's family one day. We gathered our things to leave, and he yelled to me, "I'm driving!" Given that he had been drinking all day, I suggested to him that it would be better if I drove since he was drunk. He looked back at me with this blank stare and said, "Get your ass in the car." Not wanting to make a scene in front of family and friends, I obliged and loaded the kids into the car. As he drove off, we entered an on-ramp to go over a bridge, when he started swerving in the car. I asked him to pull over and offered to take the wheel again. He just looked over at me and said, "I will kill all of us in this car." I pleaded with him not to do that and asked yet again if I could drive. He ignored me and pressed the gas pedal. I looked over and noticed that his speed was over one hundred miles per hour. Then he asked, "Are you ready to die?" Not sure if it was from me or a spirit that came over me, I answered, "If you going to do it, just fucking do it." He looked back at me and said, "Oh, now you have courage?" I didn't say a word or look in his direction. I just closed my eyes and started praying:

Dear Lord, I know I have not done things in the way you wanted me to, but I come to you in need of your strength. I am tired of living like this. Please give me the strength, courage, and wisdom to walk away for good. I know I have nothing to my name, but I have faith you will make a way out of no way and provide for me and my boys. In Jesus's name, amen.

As we arrived at the house, Thomas yelled, "I'm going to get you when we get inside!" I was ready for his ass this time. I took the kids and locked us in the room. In true Thomas fashion, he was right behind me. He began beating on the door, telling me to open it, and I yelled, "No!" Next, he started kicking the door until he busted it open. He swung to punch me in the face, and it was as if a switch turned on inside my body and I was in full fight mode. It was as if I became a boxer. I ducked his punches and kicked him straight in the balls. He fell to his knees, and I just started swinging.

I swung with my fists and anything I could grab. It seemed that as soon as he saw me fight back, he got up and left me alone. I will say, that was the first time in a long time I had a peaceful night's rest.

The next morning, I woke up energized and happy. I found Thomas sleeping in the living room and woke his ass up and told him to "get the fuck out of my house." He rolled his eyes and stated, "I'm not leaving . . . I live here too." See, he was only street smart, but I was street smart and book smart. I told him, "Your name is not on shit in here. Not the lights, water, gas, or the house. You are not legally allowed to have anything but a visit, and right now you are trespassing. So *get the fuck out!* He said, "Where will I go?" I said, "I don't give a damn where you go. You can go by a bitch, family, shelter, or church, I don't care, but you got to get the hell out of here!" He packed whatever stuff he could grab and made his way to the door. He looked back and asked, "Can I come by later to get the rest of my things?" I replied, "Naw, that shit will be at the nearest Goodwill."

When I closed the door, I felt that not only had I regained my voice, I was at peace. It was just my boys and me. I didn't care whether I could pay any of my bills or where our next meal would come from. I was happy to be me and free. There is no better feeling than to be free from a person who tormented you. But was I?

Leaving Thomas for good was the best decision of my life. However, even though I was free from the relationship, I was not truly free. I found out that leaving an abusive situation is a process. Often, your abuser finds other ways to inflict on you. Well, in my case, Thomas knew, or thought he knew, what could hurt me and cause me to come running back. Money. That's right, the oldest trick in the book. He decided that if we weren't together, I was on my own with the kids, with no support from him. However, I never looked back.

Over the next couple of months, I tried to keep a normal routine by going to work every day. Still confused by my next steps, I continued to pray every day. It felt as if my mind was going through a detox process. As women, we have the tendency to replay our relationship from start to finish over and over in our heads. It's as if we are trying to analyze, then reanalyze, the situation. We even feel as though God doesn't hear us, but I am here to tell you that, in my case, He heard me, but I was just too damn stubborn to listen. I asked God why He let me go through all of this. Why was I born into a life filled with pain? Then I noticed that one minute, I was questioning Him, while the next minute, I was begging for forgiveness. I realized that going through this detox process was God's way of rebuilding me. This process didn't involve me being in a church, but rather in a room, crying my heart out and having that conversation with God, letting him know I was ready to receive Him and be molded the right way.

Chapter Eight

Redemption

eing in a relationship for that long with all of the pain I endured, took me on a rollercoaster in which I had a lot healing to do. I found that I needed to deconstruct myself and put myself back together again. I had to figure out who is Keisha and what are things I liked and wanted. Just defining what happiness looks like for me. One of the first things I did was simply stand in front of the mirror to fully see myself. Then I smiled at myself and thought about all the things I been through and yet I am still here. Of course, the next thing was to blast Mary J. Blige's "My Life" album throughout the house with a glass of wine. Something about her albums get your mindset to a place of peace. I have always believed music to be therapeutic since I was in the high school band.

Music to me was like hearing someone go through the same situation and overcoming the same thing. Healing is a long process that doesn't happen overnight and can't be rushed. Don't get mad at yourself and have patience. I adopted a habit of meditation just to remind myself that my trauma wasn't my fault. I also sought out professional help from a therapist to help deal with the anger and rage I was feeling inside. Talking to someone was one of the ways I discovered my own identity. Along with my therapy sessions, I created my own set of rules for myself to live by:

1. Keep people in your circle that add value to you and not drama. The old saying blood is thicker than water don't mean it was referring to family. Sometimes God sends the right people in your pathway to help you along your journey. Cherish those people. I know the lord sent me several people that I am forever grateful for.

2. Look in the mirror every day and tell yourself "You can have whatever you want." I found telling myself yes was motivation. Being with Thomas I was always in a state of fear so telling myself yes gave me a sense of empowerment.

Also, I learn to accept the things I went through didn't happen to break me but to build me into the person I was destined to be. Not only did I go through a physical and mental detox, but also a spiritual one. Some of those things made me a better leader professionally, a better mother, and a mentor to people.

I now volunteer with youth programs and help at risk youth make better life choices.

Again, this process was far from easy. I will say this: when you walk away from drama, good things happen. Everything was changing so fast it was surreal. The next two years were extremely hard. Juggling life as a single mom of three took a toll on me. I learned to suppress my emotional needs so I could just focus on taking us out of poverty. My priorities were my career and my kids. I'd figured the best revenge I could get on anyone that wronged me was to become successful.

Within three years, I accomplished things I thought I could only dream of. I graduated from college and created a successful career. I finally moved to Atlanta for good where I also completed by bachelor's degree. I obtained the job of my dreams working for one of the most renown organizations in the state of Georgia. As for Thomas, I left him in New Orleans doing who knows what. Co-parenting was non-existent just like any financial support. He called or texted the kids every now and then. At first it was frustrating not receiving any help, but just like the old saying, "Momma's Baby, Daddy's maybe." My faith in God put me in the position to support myself and the kids without any help from

Thomas. My kids and I were now in a position where we had everything we wanted, with no worries. Hell, I even started dating again. I met a man when I least expected it. God said he would send somebody that was right for us. This man goes by the name Henry. I met Henry at a gas station as I was getting ready to pump gas into my car. As I got ready to open my gas tank, I heard a man approaching, saying, "Excuse me, ma'am, can I talk to you for a second?" I turned around and saw a fine, caramel, sexy-ass man coming closer. As he reached me, he said, "What's a pretty woman like you doing pumping your own gas?" I just laughed. "A car needs gas to drive, right? So, I have to put gas in the car." Based on the look on his face, he caught my feisty attitude, but it didn't deter him. He just smiled and said, "How about I make you a deal. I will pay for your gas and pump if I can have your number and we can go out sometime."

Hesitant, I politely agreed to the deal. I thought to myself, *Now, my car's fuel gauge is on empty, so let's see if he still wants to go on a date after he sees my car takes premium and has a thirty-gallon tank.* Sure enough, Henry filled up my tank, and as soon as I drove off, he called my phone. Being skeptical of this man, I still accepted his offer to meet up and have dinner. We met at a little cozy restaurant in the Atlanta area called Canoe. As I walked into the restaurant, I could see him waiting at the bar. We let the hostess know we were ready for our table. As we sat down for dinner, I couldn't help but notice that not only was he easy on the eyes, but he had a damn brain. There is nothing like a man you can have an intelligent conversation with.

Within months, Henry and I were inseparable. However, I still had all my defenses up. I did not want to end up in another Thomas situation after finding my peace. At first, dating him was difficult. I had become too afraid to let any man get close to me after what I had gone through. Allowing yourself to be vulnerable is easier said than done. However, he wasn't anything like Thomas—of course, but I did background checks on him as if I was the damn NSA—and I wasn't going to make him pay for me being with a narcissistic, abusive man. He was a gentleman and an ultimate man's man. Ladies, he can *fix shit*! Best of all, Henry was patient and waited for me. He led by his actions and not his words. He also would politely correct me and remind me that I could be rough around the edges. But he was never mean or aggressive. When the timing felt right, I even allowed him to meet my kids.

Within a year, the walls came down, and I found myself in love with my best friend. The kind of love that lets you be one hundred percent yourself. The love he displays to my kids is as if they were his own. It seems as if I have finally found someone that loves me past my pain and is in it for the long haul.

Throughout my life, I have learned a lot. I have learned that what doesn't kill you strengthens you. Each one of us has something in us to preserve, even at our lowest point. You see, whether you believe it or not, your life has a purpose, and it is meaningful. Don't give up or quit. This is my time to shine, and I live by my own rules as I enter the next chapter in my life. My story is my Exodus.

Chapter Nine

Author's Reflections

Keisha's story is one that we as women can identify with far too often. Her story reminds us of different issues we have faced within our own lives, from adolescent to adulthood. The manifestation of abandonment issues started in her childhood. The world often depicts the effects felt by males that have grown up in a broken home. However, we, as females, are affected just as much. As Keisha grows into a young girl, she experiences traumatic events in which she did not have emotional support from anyone. This laid the groundwork for a vicious cycle of self-hate, fear, and anxiety. Then there were trust issues. By the time she reached her teenage years, they grew into her seeking validation from the streets.

We all know how the street life works. We exit a bad situation at home only to subject ourselves to the real danger that awaits. Sometimes it shows a false sense of the way the world works. Depending on which turn you take, you can hit a chain of unfortunate events. For a while, this was Keisha's path. She struggled to find herself, which led to her vulnerability to Thomas's manipulation, control, and abuse. I am glad she found the courage to rise above the cycle of abuse and get out of her situation before it was too late. Often, domestic violence is overlooked until it's too late for the victim. Keisha's story is one that I hope will serve as a reminder that, as women, regardless of what shade we are, we are one. And it's never too late to reclaim your life and live it to its fullest potential.

A Poem for All the Women for Whom Keisha Is You

Hey, Girl

Hey, Girl, I see you
Dry your eyes. I know you're tired
Tired of the disappointment and struggles
Tired of the mental and physical abuse taking its toll
Don't know whether today is the day you fold
Fold from the pressures this world can bring
But you know you have children depending on you so you
can't bring your life to an end
Hey, Girl, I see you
Realizing it is not worth it and pain is just a feeling that will pass
God said stick with Him and his plans will forever last
Hey, Girl, I see you
Hey, Girl, I see you
Do you know you are that Girl?
You are that girl that rose from the concrete
Who holds her head up high through it all
Huh
And even though you struggled, you did not break or fall
You are not defined by the pains and trauma you endured
But by the grace and humility of a soul that is pure
We see your growth, shining so bright
Telling your story, letting other women know it will be all right
Hey, Girl, I see you
Hey, Girl, we see you
And we love you